DECAY

JOE SCIPIONE

D & T
PUBLISHING

For Mandy

ACKNOWLEDGMENTS

This is the first book in a series I'm calling the Contact Series. I've always enjoyed learning and teaching about the Civil War and I knew someday I'd write a Civil War book. After writing this book, I realized there was a lot more to the story. If you like Decay keep your eye out of the rest of the books in the series as they come out, I think you'll like them. Writing a book is a solitary activity but it takes a lot of people working together to publish one. A million thanks to everyone who helped make this book possible. My publishers Dawn and Tim have been helpful and supportive through the entire process. Don Noble for creating an incredible cover that really captures the heart of this story. Patrick C. Harrison III for making finding all of the mistakes I made along the way. Dave LaSota for reading an early version of this and always giving some great advice. Philip Fracassi, Steve Stred and John Durgin for their incredibly kind words about this book. Mandy, Tom and Isabella for putting up with me and letting me get into the writing zone one or two times a day. I couldn't have done this without them. Most of all thanks to you, the reader, for picking up this book and giving my weird, scary story a shot. I hope you like it.

Joe Scipione
September 2022

1

IT WAS his first time with a woman; he loved her, but he was going to cause of her death. His mouth pressed against hers. Their bodies writhed together, their sweat mixing. He was inside her, holding her close. His skin, covered and hidden for so long, pressed against hers. The first touch he'd felt in a long time. When Martin Quigley finished and untangled himself from Mary-Louise he knew she'd be dead within twenty-four hours.

The moment of ecstasy passed; Martin realized the price of his pleasure. He knew the effect he would have on her, knew the consequences before he decided to take her to his bed, but it had to be done, and it had to be then. He'd be fine of course, nothing ever happened to him.

Guilt overtook him. Mary-Louise curled her body next to him, draping her arm across his chest, resting her head against his shoulder. The touch was something he never got to experience. Just feeling a woman make contact with his skin after all these years was a feeling he wouldn't forget, but he didn't want to be near her. He wanted to touch her, but didn't at the same time. He knew what that touch meant. The touch was death. He wasn't used to that much human contact. Each second her skin touched his was agony; he couldn't take it. Martin got out of bed, walked to the window, stared out onto the field surrounding his small home. He remained there, naked, silent, thinking about what the future held.

"What's wrong?" she asked and pushed herself up on an elbow, still wrapped in his sheets.

Martin said nothing, shaking his head, losing himself in thought.

The room filled with silence, his head with guilt, regret, but if he was going to do it, it had to be now. There was not going to be any other time. And he'd always wanted his first time to be with Mary-Louise, but he never could go through with it because he knew the results. He didn't want his first time to be meaningless; he could have found a woman that meant nothing to him, but he couldn't bring himself to do that. He wouldn't have gone through with it. He'd loved Mary-Louise from afar for years and now he'd loved her in a much more physical way.

Martin felt her eyes on him, but kept his eyes focused on the field outside. He wasn't going to break the silence. Her breathing slowed. Martin waited, wanting her to be fast asleep before he returned to bed. He listened to her slow, heavy, rhythmic breathing and assumed she was asleep, or close to it. He waited still, giving her a few extra minutes. Finally, he turned, expecting her to be asleep, but she was still sitting up in bed watching him.

"When do you leave?" she asked.

Martin sighed, returned to bed, lifted the sheet and slid in next to her.

"Two, maybe three days. The war doesn't seem like it's going to end any time soon. Still have a hard time when I think about fighting other Americans"

"And you wanted to...you know...before you left?"

Martin nodded. "I always wanted you to be my first. I just thought there would be more time. If there was more time, it would have been different. We could have done it right. Not quick like this."

"It was perfect. I'm glad we could be together. I've always liked you Martin. Maybe, when you get back from the war, we can get married, make a family."

"I would like that," he said. It wasn't a lie. He would love to marry Mary-Louise and have a family with her. Would have loved to grow old with her in his farm house, working the fields every day and coming home to her face every night. He *would* love it, but knew there was nothing he could do for her now. There was no future for them. No future for her. She was already dead. It was his fault.

"Really?" She pulled him tight against her, he feeling her breasts press against the side of his arm. Martin wanted nothing more than to stay there like that with her. Forget the war, forget his ability and live the rest of his life like that.

Then she coughed. A small one into her balled up fist. She turned away from him to do it, then turned back to look at him again.

"You need to leave," he said.

"But—" she started. Martin wouldn't let her get the next word out. He couldn't see this. He knew that sound. He'd heard it before. Twice. The sound of those coughs haunted him and lived in his dreams. The first time he heard them through his bedroom wall. But he didn't know anything back them. He hadn't known what would happen. Those times had been purely an accident. This time, *he knew*, and touched her anyway.

"No. You need to leave now. Get the hell out of here." He ripped the covers off both of them. She reached for the sheets, trying to cover herself back up, but he'd thrown the sheets too far away and she lay there naked, exposed. He didn't want to do it, he wanted her to stay. But he couldn't watch that. Couldn't have her be there in the morning. He loved her, so she had to leave.

She coughed again, harder this time as if the first cough didn't do the job and she still had something in her lungs that she couldn't get out. She'd never be able to get it out.

"Get dressed and get the fuck out." Martin kicked her clothes over to her as she started to cry.

"What's wrong?"

"I'm not who you thought I was. You don't want to marry a man like me. Now get the hell out of here. I don't ever want to see you again."

Mary-Louise dressed in a hurry. Martin watched her, not bothering to help or get dressed himself. She left his bedroom in tears and slammed the front door when she exited the house. She coughed again as she walked down the path and in the direction of her parent's farm across town.

Tears formed in his eyes before she'd even left his room, but Martin turned away so she wouldn't see. He hated what he'd done and hated the way he treated her, but it was the only way to get her out. He didn't want her to see him like that. Her cough outside made him collapse in a naked heap of sorrow.

It was then, curled up in a ball on the floor of his bedroom, he thought back to how it all started for him, with the deaths of his parents.

2

IT WAS the worst week of his life, days he'd do anything to forget but ones that would live forever in his mind. It began like any other week. Young Martin got home from school and did his chores around the house. Usually he helped Mother, but as he got older, he was allowed to help Father out in the fields for a short time each day. Field work was hard work, but Martin liked spending time with Father and he liked helping, even if he was exhausted at the end. The hard work was worth it.

After a day at school then an afternoon helping Mother in the house and Father in the fields, Martin's body ached for bed. But when he climbed into bed that night, something didn't feel right. His hands tingled and his legs wouldn't stop moving even though he was exhausted. He wanted to tell his mother about it; she must have been able to see and hear his legs moving back and forth under the blankets, but he figured he was just tired and needed to rest his body. Besides, Father would never trouble her with something like that and Martin was becoming more like a grown-up every day.

"Goodnight, honey," Mother said just like she did every night. She sat on the edge of his bed, leaned over and gave him a kiss on the forehead, the final part of their bedtime routine.

"'Night, Mom," young Martin said. Even as he said it, he felt a tingling itch on his forehead where her lips touched him. At first, he thought it was just a momentary strange feeling up there, but when Mother sat back and looked down at him, the strange feeling persisted.

Martin resisted the urge to scratch at it, knowing she would point out the fact that he was wiping off her kiss, so he left it. He could stand it for a moment and she'd leave in a second anyway. She sat on the edge of his bed and he pretended to yawn then rolled over, his back to her. It was the sign that he was ready to fall asleep, he did it every night, usually because he *was* ready to fall asleep. Not that night though. Sure enough, after he turned, Mother got up and left. Once he heard his bedroom door close, Martin rubbed and scratched at his head to relieve the momentary discomfort. It was only momentary because even before he rubbed at it, the feeling was almost gone. After a few minutes his legs calmed down and Martin's eyes began to droop closed. At some point, he fell asleep.

He woke to the sound of her coughing. The rooms in the house were small, the walls thin. His first thought was that he had over-slept. His eyes darted to the window, but when he saw the sky was dark, absent even pf the light-blue glow of early-morning, he knew something was wrong. The coughs were intermittent, but violent. A few soft muted coughs, followed by a loud hack and a groan that seemed to cause his mother actual pain. Between them, his father's voice. It was low and muffled, Martin couldn't make out the words, but could tell from the tone he was trying to console mother. Martin could imagine him, sitting on the edge of the bed beside her, rubbing her back as she worked through one harsh cough after another.

The coughs didn't stop. Martin knew better than to leave his room before it was time to get up, so he laid there; as far as his parents knew he was asleep. But the coughs worsened. By morning each cough was hard and loud, with barely enough time in-between for mother to catch her breath.

Martin left his room around the time he was supposed to and

prepared himself for school. He was worried for his mother, but had to get away from the sound of her coughs. They only made him worry more.

"What's happening?" Martin asked when his father stepped out of his parent's bedroom. Through the briefly open door he saw his mother sitting on the edge of the bed just like he'd pictured, pale and weak. His father quickly pulled the door shut when he noticed Martin looking past him. He didn't know then, but this would be the last time he saw her.

"Your mother just doesn't feel well today, Martin. I've already sent for the doctor. He should be along shortly. But there's nothing to worry about," his father said. His words showed no cause for concern, but the look on his face told a different story. "Run off to school and she'll be better when you get home."

His father knelt down and gave Martin a hug. Martin wrapped his arms around the man's neck and they held each other tightly for a moment, Martin's cheek pressed against his father's. Martin said goodbye, left the house and made the walk to school. Again, there was a lingering itch this time on his cheek, part of him wondering if his father would be coughing when he got home from school.

The house was silent when he got home later that day. Father wasn't there, but Aunt Mary, his mother's sister, told him the terrible news. His mother had passed away around the middle of the day. To make it worse, his father, it seemed, had contracted the same disease that killed his mother. Father was being quarantined at home and Martin was to remain with his aunt and uncle until he could be examined and declared safe for the community. They were worried, Aunt Mary told him, that it was some new kind of plague. Martin's heart raced, beads of sweat formed on the back of his neck and, though he wanted to cry, nothing happened. He absently rubbed his forehead. Mother had touched him there and he'd felt that strange itch or tingle; the next thing he knew she was coughing then dead. Then father touched him, on his cheek this time, now father was sick. The urge to cry was there and Martin held off as long as he could, he looked up at Aunt Mary with tears in his eyes, but thought maybe it would be best not to touch her. He fled from the house instead, crying alone in the middle of the corn field.

Father died early the next morning. Martin guessed—but wasn't sure—he'd caused their deaths. He hoped it was just a strange coincidence. He wanted to test his theory.

With both parents dead he went to live with Aunt Mary, her husband and his cousins. They also had a cat. It wasn't the worst cat in the world—it certainly didn't deserve to die—but Martin figured killing a cat was better than killing a human. If he *had* caused his parents death, he wanted to know for sure, though he might not be able to live with himself if it was true. If he didn't cause their death, he needed to know that too.

He made an effort not to touch anyone. It wasn't too difficult actually. They wouldn't let him attend either of his parent's funerals because he was too young, which would have involved lots of hugs and kisses from family and strangers alike. Martin was fine with that. He said goodbye to them in his own way. Because of the grief, most people stayed away from him, probably because they didn't know how to talk to him about what happened.

The cat though, Silver, followed Martin everywhere. Martin refrained from patting it for a while, just in case, but he had to know. One day when his cousins, aunt and uncle were either too busy to notice or out of the house, Martin decided to finally go through with the experiment he thought up in his head. He hated to do it, but it needed to be done.

He sat on the floor with his back against the wall and the cat, who was never far away from Martin, climbed up and sat on his lap. Martin stroked the cat's fur, feeling the smooth coat under his hand. It was actually a comforting feeling. But Martin thought the fur might insulate the cat from his touch and he needed to know for sure. So, he put his hand by the cat's mouth.

The cat sniffed at his hand, as cats do, then began to lick. First it was one lick and then a second and third. The tongue was rough compared to its soft grey fur. The lapping at his hand went on another few minutes and Gabe, his older cousin walked by, laughed at him and then carried on with his day. Martin had hoped no one would see him with the cat, especially if it was found dead the next day, but that plan was ruined. He could only hope Gabe didn't make the connection. He let the cat have a few more licks, then stood up and shooed it away. He didn't notice the tingles, but it was hard to tell because of the cat's rough tongue.

Aunt Mary found the cat in front of the house the next day. They buried it in the front yard.

3

"I KNOW WHAT YOU ARE," Gabe said as they walked along the road from town. The rest of the family was up ahead—Aunt Mary, Uncle Hatch and the younger girls—unable to hear them. Martin and Gabe were the only two boys in the family other than Uncle Hatch, and most people assumed they were best friends, with Gabe taking on the role of older brother.

It wasn't that Martin disliked Gabe; he had always been nice to him. But he saw the look of pity on Gabe's face when he looked at Martin and it was hard to feel very close to a person who looked at you that way. Whether it was true or not, Martin figured Gabe looked at him as the orphan his family took in and not as an actual brother.

"What do you mean you know what I am?" Martin felt his heart drop, but pretended to have no idea. Martin knew what he was, but there was no way Gabe could know. Even with what happened with the cat, it was just a coincidence. It had happened three times now and Martin only half-believed it himself. There was no way Gabe could know unless he'd been there when his parents died. Even then, Gabe wouldn't have been able to put it all together.

"You know what I mean. Your mother. Your father. And I saw you with the cat."

"I—I don't—"

"You do too. I can see it in your eyes. Don't worry, I won't say anything. It's probably not your fault anyway. You can't control it. At least you don't seem like the kind of person who would do something like that on purpose." Gabe walked next to him, but there was a noticeable space between them. There wasn't going to be any incidental contact.

"No," Martin sighed. He'd have to reveal his secret. "I didn't know that was going to happen to the cat. I—I was just testing it out to see, Gabe, honest." He didn't mean to, or want to, or even know it was coming on, but out of nowhere, he cried.

"It's okay. How does it work?"

"I don't know really. I think I just touch someone. Or something alive." Martin said, wiping tears from his cheeks.

"Really? That's all there is to it?"

"Yeah, I guess. I don't really know. I touched my...my mom and she got sick that night, well she touched me on the forehead. I had this weird tingly feeling after that. I didn't connect it. Then my dad touched me on the cheek, his to mine, and I felt that strange feeling again. Next thing I know..." Martin trailed off, trying to stop the tears welling up in his eyes.

"And the cat was just so you would know for sure."

Martin looked up at his cousin, vision blurred, and nodded. They slowed their pace, his Aunt and Uncle and the girls walking further ahead of them.

"Listen, it's not necessarily a bad thing. It wasn't your fault your parents died; you didn't know. Believe it or not, Grandma told me we've had stuff like this happened in our family before. I don't know much more than that. She didn't really get specific, but I don't think you're the only one."

"I never met Grandma. She really said that?" Martin said. The only thing he knew was that she died when he was not even one year old. His mother told him about her. The shock of what Gabe said, stopped the tears. At least he knew he wasn't alone, even if he felt alone.

"Yeah, but she was saying a lot of crazy things at the end. If it's true I don't even think my mother, or yours, knew about it. Just one of the crazy things she was saying toward the end. I didn't think much of it until the cat died after I saw you with it the other day."

They walked in silence. Martin didn't know what to think. But he felt comforted to know he might not be the only one. Not that he would ever be able to know for sure. He wasn't going to ever bring it up with anyone. It was too dangerous. He didn't like Gabe knowing his secret, but there was nothing he could do. Why was Gabe telling him all this? His mind wandered and he thought about his parents again. If he knew about his ability a month ago, he could have stopped his mother from kissing him. If he'd known he could have stopped the whole thing. But his life had changed, and he would have to live the rest of his life knowing he killed both his parents.

"But listen," Gabe said, the rest of the family out of sight, "it's not really a bad thing, like I was saying. I mean, you're a weapon. You don't need to carry a sword or knife or gun with you. You are the weapon. If people knew, they would keep their distance."

"I don't want that; I just want to be me."

"I know you do, Martin. But you'll never be a normal kid again." Gabe smiled and looked down at Martin as they walked.

Martin didn't know what to think of Gabe after that. He trusted Gabe with his secret, but hated the words he'd used to describe him. *You'll never be a normal kid again.*

They didn't talk the rest of the way home, but Martin's mind wouldn't stop. He was only six years old. He shouldn't have had to lose both his parents. He shouldn't have to live with himself knowing he was the reason they died. It wasn't something a child his age was supposed to deal with. But that was his life now. He knew what he knew and he was going to have to grow up fast. He had the responsibility to keep people from touching him. He vowed that afternoon walking up to the house with Gabe that he'd never use his special ability on purpose for as long as he lived. He was going to be normal and it would take a lot of work for that to happen.

4

It took a lot of work but Martin grew up and lived as normal as he could, given the situation. He wasn't totally normal; he took to wearing gloves so he didn't accidentally touch anyone, he withdrew, especially from family because he knew if he got too close to them emotionally, they might try to hug him or joke around and make contact with him by accident. But he kept Gabe's words in the back of his head—always. He was going to be as normal as his situation would allow and show Gabe that it could be done. Gabe, in spite of his assertion that Martin would never be normal, became the person in his life that he was closest with. Gabe was the only person he could share things with; the only person in Martin's life who really understood why he was the way he was. It might have been a family secret, or just specific to him because his grandmother had just been raving mad by that point, but Martin wasn't going to let it ruin his life. He was going to be normal and live in spite of his ability—or was it his curse.

Even though he was close with his older cousin, Gabe could torment Martin from time to time as an older sibling might do, which Gabe had become by default. It was Gabe who gave him the nickname that followed him around the rest of his life, and the one

Martin never wanted anything to do with—Decay. Martin was thirteen and had lived with his Aunt, Uncle and cousins longer than he'd lived with his parents by then. He still felt like an outsider, and assumed he always would.

Not far from their house there was a pond that Gabe used to go with his friends when he was younger to swim and avoid school during the week and work on the farm with his father on the weekends. Gabe always asked Martin to go with him, but Martin refused. He didn't want to be around Gabe's friends was always his excuse. Then one day, Gabe asked him and told him his friends wouldn't be going, that it would be just the two of them. With his built-in excuse gone, Martin struggled to find a reason not to go and begrudgingly agreed to join Gabe. They left the house early before anyone else was awake, grabbed some food from the kitchen they hoped Aunt Mary wouldn't miss and left before sunrise.

Even though it was a hot summer morning, Martin was covered head to toe, including boots and, as always, his gloves. For a while people questioned him about the gloves, tight and dark and leather. He had two pair, one black, which his aunt and uncle got him when he asked one day, and the other dark brown, having belonged to his father. Shortly after his parents died when he first started wearing gloves, he dreamed of one day having hands large enough to fit in them. As he got older, his hands grew into the gloves until it got to the point where he could wear them comfortably and actually be able to do things with his hands.

The walk to the pond with Gabe wasn't so bad. There were worse things Martin could think of to do on a Sunday morning. Through some tall grass, across a field, weaving through a small wooded area, and they were there. Within ten minutes of their arrival, Gabe had stripped down to his underwear and jumped in the lake. Martin stood on the shore, sweating and looking down at the refreshing water.

"Come on Martin, jump in. Live a little," Gabe shouted as he lay on his back and kicked across the water.

"I can't."

"Sure, you can. Just take off all those layers and hop in."

"No, I can't," he said but he wanted to feel the water more than anything. "What if something happens?"

"Nothing's going to happen, come on. I know about you. I won't get anywhere near you. Just come in. If it's not fun you can get out and we can go back home and pull weeds if you want."

Martin always hated when people said stuff like that because it meant they knew it was going to be fun. Gabe was the master at it. He already knew the answer and was just trying to get him to do whatever it was he wanted Martin to do. It had been like that his whole life. People constantly tried to get him to do things even though he told them he had no interest in it. Of course, he wanted to do those things. He wanted to do everything: spend time with friends, run off with kids his age and have an adventure the adults in their lives would disapprove of, get close to a girl, kiss a girl. He wanted to do all of those things, but couldn't. And never did. He'd missed out on a fun childhood protecting those around him from himself. They didn't know they needed protecting, but he did and he couldn't be the cause of another meaningless death.

This felt different to Martin. It *was* different. Gabe wasn't like the others. Gabe knew the risks. Martin didn't have to protect him. If something happened, Martin would still feel guilty. Gabe may drive him crazy sometimes, but Martin always thought he had his best interests at heart. Maybe he was doing this so he *could* have a normal life. Gabe could protect himself and Martin needed to trust him, at least this one time.

After a few more minutes of sweating in the sun and Gabe's continued goading, Martin stood up and stripped down to his underwear. He stood at the edge of the pond, his bare feet touching grass for the first time in years. A bush brushed against his leg and he bent down and touched it. Martin smiled, feeling the cool smooth leaves against his sensory deprived hands. He rubbed the leaf with his thumb, feeling its smooth surface against his skin.

"Just stay back, okay?" Martin said. He stepped forward, his feet submerging into the lukewarm water.

Gabe, who was already at least thirty feet away swam back another twenty feet to give Martin a wide berth.

"This good enough?' Gabe asked.

Martin couldn't tell if he was joking or not. He actually wished Gabe would back up another twenty feet or even get out of the water, but he didn't say anything, just nodded and contemplated his next action.

Then, with a wide smile growing on his face, Martin leapt into the air, let out a howl and splashed down into the water. He swam and splashed and had more fun in the water with Gabe than he'd had since the day his mother got sick.

They stayed at the pond all day. Gabe got out of the water a few times but Martin stayed in, enjoying the feeling of being outside and uncovered. For first time since he learned of his secret, he felt like a regular, *normal* kid.

The sun rose, passed overhead and threatened to drop lower in the sky. Gabe was in the water with Martin and looked up first, recognizing the time.

"Sun's starting to drop down a little, we need to start thinking about heading back you know."

Martin nodded. He understood but didn't want the day to end. He didn't want to go back to covering himself, staying away from others, being not normal.

"I'm gonna go dry off and get my clothes back on, you should get out too," Gabe said as he made for shore.

Martin decided to make one more lap around the edge of the pond then join Gabe and get ready to head back. He only took about ten strokes when Gabe interrupted him.

"Holy shit, Martin. Look at this!"

"What is it?" He lifted his head up out of the water and looked in Gabe's direction. Martin pushed the hair out of his eyes but still couldn't see what he was looking at so he swam over to his cousin.

"Come here. Wow. You won't believe it. Well, maybe you won't."

Martin got closer, swimming first, then putting his feet down and walking toward the shoreline. The water held him back but he dragged his legs forward, watching Gabe to see what he was looking at. He blinked water out of his eyes and everything blurry became clear. Martin felt his heart drop like it had when he first discovered his strange ability.

"Shit." Martin stared at the circle of dead grass Gabe stood in the middle of. "Back up."

Gabe said nothing but took a few steps back, away from the edge to avoid any contact.

"I killed it all. And this bush too." Martin touched the leafless bush he'd felt when he first got in the water. The touch of his finger caused the dead, rotten branch to fall to the ground.

"It's decaying right before our eyes. I—I mean I knew what you could do. I just never expected to see it like this." Gabe backed away, shook his head and finished getting dressed.

Martin studied the bush and the dead grass and dressed in silence. The two did not speak another word the rest of the way back home.

The next day, Gabe told Martin he was going to call him Decay from then on. Martin hated the name, but considering the circumstances thought it was fitting.

5

MARTIN PEELED himself off his bedroom floor. Mary-Louise was gone. He'd never see her alive again. The next day there would be word of her death, but the day after that he was off to fight in the war between the states. Based on what he knew about the battles and engagements, there was a chance he'd never return to Milford again, destined to be buried somewhere in the western or southern states next to Union and Confederate soldiers.

The combination of guilt over Mary-Louise and self-pity over his childhood left Martin exhausted. He never slept without being covered head to toe, but didn't have the energy to get dressed and collapsed into bed naked, hoping no one would be there shaking him when he awoke.

Martin rarely dreamed, but when he did, he dreamed of his parents. The only dreams he ever had involved them. He preferred not to dream because the dreams of his mother and father always ended with him sitting up in bed, shouting and sweating. When he slept that night, he saw their faces, his mother's first, the last time he saw her when she placed that kiss upon his deadly flesh. Then his father's, when his attempt to console a worried son cost the man his life. After that, there were no images in his dream. Just the black nothingness of sleep and of coughs echoing, growing in volume until he woke to a damp bed drenched in sweat.

Martin dressed and checked the time; almost twelve hours since Mary-Louise left. She would be confined to bed by this point, coughing, well on the way to her grave. Martin pushed the thought aside. He didn't have time to think about that .He left for war in one day.

He wasn't the only one in town leaving to fight and without much to do other than be at the train station at the appointed time, the group of conscripted men decided to get acquainted.

Martin left the house to meet the others at the town common. He wished Gabe had been around. For as much as his older cousin had tormented him growing up and given him the horrible nickname, it would have been good to have someone to talk to. Gabe left town five years earlier after getting married. His new father-in-law had two-hundred acres of farmland in Western Massachusetts and needed help. Gabe was more than able to do the work, having worked the family farm in Milford most of his life and there was a lot of money to be made in that part of the state due to its quick development. Gabe would be crazy not to take his new family up on the offer to buy-in and help out, so he left. Martin understood, but missed him from time to time.

The day was warm but Martin donned his gloves, boots and long sleeves as always; the only skin showing was around his face. He knew he'd recognize most of the others leaving, but wouldn't know their names. They would all know him, mostly because of his unique nickname, but didn't think of any of them as close friends.

"There's Decay," a man Martin recognized said as he approached the small group gathered at the middle of the town common.

As he expected, all the faces were familiar but he only knew a few names. Because of his ability, Martin tended to shy away from social situations. When he did find himself at one, he remained on the fringes, standing by himself, talking to as few people as possible until it was acceptable for him to leave. He recognized John Baxter, James Short and William Arthur; the rest he didn't know by name. Thanks to Gabe and the nickname he'd given him, Martin stuck out despite his desire to blend in; they all knew him as soon as he walked up.

It hadn't taken long for the name to spread. Gabe told Martin not to worry because no one would have been able to figure out how he got the name, even if he was truthful, no one would believe it. Martin understood, but he still didn't like to be called that name. By the time he decided that though, the name had spread and stuck. From then on, he was Decay everywhere he went.

The men introduced themselves. Martin used his real name when he made his introduction and greeted everyone with a gloved hand, but they all responded with a joking line about how everyone calls him Decay. He laughed along with them and let them continue calling him whatever they liked. The less problems with this group, the better.

They didn't have a plan for the meeting. It wasn't official. Other than the fact that they were meeting at the train station bright and early the next day, there wasn't much to talk about. They discussed the war, their thoughts on secession and slavery, and where they thought they would end up.

There were multiple Massachusetts companies in the army, one man reported, and there was a good chance they would be split up between the different companies. The government didn't want to have all the young men from the same town killed at the same time. It would look bad, he said. Martin didn't know if that were true or not, but it made sense. In that case however, there was little reason for him to be meeting with any of these men. If they were going to be fighting together for the next eighteen months, it made sense to get to know them, grow closer to them, but if they were going to take the train to New York—from there down to Washington or west to Ohio—and be split up, it didn't much matter if they were friends or not. After a few more minutes of talking, Martin readied himself to leave, go home, finish packing and do whatever he could to keep his mind off Mary-Louise.

Martin made a few parting comments about seeing the men the next day and started to back away from the group, the men nodded, smiled and continued their conversation so Martin turned to leave. It was typical of his life. He'd slip away, unnoticed and wouldn't be missed.

He was only a few steps away from the group when someone called out.

"Martin, wait up," the voice said. Martin turned and saw John Baxter had left the group and was walking in his direction. Because Martin grew so much more than he consumed on his farm, he sold most of his crop. The Baxter family owned the general store in town and bought most of Martin's excess crop. Martin knew most members of the family and more often than not, he made his sales to John Baxter. Martin's surplus was high so his prices were low and the store always bought from him. Over the years, he developed a friendly, working relationship with John.

"Hey, John, I'm headed out. There's a lot to get done and we're not really doing anything here."

"I agree, I'm leaving too. Figured I'd walk with you."

John lived on the same side of town as Martin and the walk back would keep them together for a couple of miles before John would turn left and Martin continue on to his home.

"Sure, no problem," Martin said and then turned and continued on his way. John fell in step next to him.

The walk was fast. They talked business most of the way. John had family that would be able to take over his duties while he was gone. Martin had no family that was close and hired out someone he knew and trusted from town. He was instructing the man to sell all of the crops to Baxter's General Store, so it should be a good situation for both of them.

As they got closer to John's turn-off, he slowed his pace and put a hand on Martin's shoulder. Martin flinched at the touch and took a step away, hoping John didn't notice.

"Listen, Martin, I heard you back there,"

Martin frowned, unsure what John was getting at.

"You introduced yourself as Martin, not Decay. Must be tough having a nickname you don't like. I don't know if we will end up together in this war or not; if we do or if we don't, I won't use that name."

"Oh, it's okay. I'm used to it by now."

"If you don't mind me asking, what's the meaning behind it anyway?"

"Oh, I don't know." Martin felt his face flush like it always did when anyone asked that question. "My older cousin made it up when I was younger. It just kind of stuck."

He felt like telling John the truth. It must have been a mix of the sorrow he felt over the now close-to-death Mary-Louise and the time spent reminiscing the night before. Martin opened his mouth to say it, as if his heart controlled his muscles. Then he closed his mouth and let the silence between them remain empty. He hoped John hadn't seen him about to let the secret out.

"I know how older cousins can be," John laughed. "Had an older brother and cousin that are the same age. We all worked together at the store when we were younger and they were brutal to me at times. It's all part of growing up, I guess. Someone is bound to pick on the younger ones."

Martin laughed with him. "Yes. He's a good guy now, but was not so good when we were younger. Always on my case about this or that. But you're probably right, it's part of growing up and probably makes us stronger in the long run."

They continued their walk in silence and approached the turn-off toward John's house.

"Well, I guess I will see you on the train in the morning," John said.

"I will be there. I wonder how much of that is true about all of us not being together."

"Well, can't be too sure about rumors like that. But I do think Massachusetts has a lot of companies. There is no reason to believe we would all be together, but if we are, it would be an honor to fight alongside you."

"Likewise. It was good talking to you, John. See you in the morning."

They shook hands, John with his naked hand, Martin with his gloved one, then went on their way.

6

_____

"Are you ready for this?" Martin looked over at John as they crouched down behind a small rock wall on a wooded hill somewhere in Kentucky. They'd ended up in the same company, the only two men from Milford to end up together, and Martin was glad he was with John. They'd fought together, seen friends die together by the end of their first summer at war. They lived in close quarters, cried together during the cold winter months and fought side-by-side hoping for an end to the war. They no longer had a friendly working relationship; Martin wouldn't even say they were as close as brothers. They were closer than that; close in a way that only those who fought together would ever understand.

"Not ready, but I have to be." John nodded, checked the sight on his rifle and patted his belt, feeling for the metal of the bayonet. They both hoped the bayonets would still be hanging there when the fight was over.

They didn't know when the Confederate advance was coming, just that the Rebs were close by and they needed to be ready when the attack did come.

According to the scouts, a large regiment of Rebs was just down the slope below them. Colonel Chambers said the most likely attack was going to be straight up the hill, right at them. Martin looked to his right and left, some of them close friends, others men he only had lukewarm feelings for. But whether he liked them or not, he trusted them with his life. There were Rebels at the bottom of the hill. They were people but they were more than that. To Martin and John and everyone else at the top of the hill, there was death at the bottom of the hill too. Every engagement, even the successful ones, ended in death. There were soldiers who survived, but when the battle was over, death was all that remained.

"We have the high ground. This wall isn't all that bad," Martin said and he tapped the rock in front of him with his rifle, showing John just how solid their cover was. They both smiled and nodded, but also knew that half of their bodies were exposed above the wall even if they laid down flat against the ground. The wall provided some cover, but not much. Though they were on top of a hill— the high ground would help the overall outcome of the battle, but did little for them personally—still, half of the men standing with them would be dead when the fighting was over. It was the way things worked in the war between the states. Martin tried not to pay attention to the politics of it. Politically, it was a war to maintain the union and a war about slavery, but for those fighting it, it was a war of two different things: violence and death.

"Men," Colonel Chambers shouted as he walked back and forth behind the line, "General Riggs is back there watching and he's almost sure the first wave of Rebel attacks are coming right up this hill. We've been through this enough times to know what to expect. You're going to hear 'em before you see 'em. Either way, you gotta be ready for 'em."

The men knocked the butts of their rifles against the dirt or the rocks of the wall in front of them in reply. Chambers nodded and continued.

"Hold your fire when you see 'em. Hold it when they stop and fire. After their first volley, we fire. Push 'em back down the hill and hope they don't come back. If they do, we do it all over again. Questions?"

He stopped and looked back and forth across the line for anyone with actual questions. There were never any questions. It was a straightforward position defense; they all knew what they were doing.

They maintained their positions and settled in for the wait. They knew what should happen, but it didn't mean it would occur the way they expected. It also didn't mean they knew *when* it was going to happen. They'd sat in a line like that for two days before an attack once. The timing of the attack was out of their hands, the only thing they could do was be ready when it came. The sun dropped lower in the sky; mid-afternoon became late afternoon.

"Rebs probably waiting for more reinforcements to arrive before they come," John speculated.

Martin nodded. There would be no fighting overnight. The men would stay on the line, sleep, and ready to fight at a moment's notice.

As the sun set further, Martin felt the entire group around him relax, the tension gone from the air. Before long, the men would be asleep. The morning air would be pregnant with tension again, but for now all was calm.

Martin and John spoke no more words as the world darkened around them. Neither was pegged to stand watch, and before long Martin was asleep, certain John was not far behind him.

They woke to the sound of gunfire.

It was close by, but not directed at them. It was dark, the sun a thought in the future, but the black of the night sky had been replaced by the glowing teal of early morning.

"That's not at us," Chambers said from somewhere behind them. "We got word of troop movement overnight. Still a bunch of 'em down the hill from us here, but they're moving off to our right too, hitting the line further down. Riggs thinks they are trying to weaken the middle then attack here to flank us and take over this position. They won't get past us though, no matter how weak the middle is. We'll make it so it doesn't matter what happens anywhere else. Control what you can control, men."

Martin blinked a few times and moved all of his body parts to make sure they were still working. He pushed himself up from laying to kneeling on all fours and then worked himself to his feet. At each stage, his bones creaked and cracked, doing what they could to protest the movement. Sleeping on the ground was horrible, but getting your body going the next morning was worse.

They waited most of the morning. Runners came through with food. It wasn't much but it would keep them going the rest of the day. It was more than the Rebs would eat that day,

Around noon they heard movement in the trees in front of them, Chambers yelled a warning and the men watched, waited, readied themselves for death, or the sight of it.

"Here we go. You ready, Decay?" John said, a grin on his face.

"Bad enough you've got all these people calling me that. You don't have to do it too." Martin laughed with his friend in spite of what lay ahead for both of them. John had let the name slip one night by mistake, and just like back home, the name stuck. Once again, Martin was Decay and there was nothing he could do about it. The good news was, just like back home, no one, not even his close friend John Baxter, knew how he got the name.

John winked back at him then sighted down the barrel of his rifle in the direction of the Rebel Army. They were down there, ghosts at the moment, but soon they would show themselves and the 21st Massachusetts was ready for them.

The rustling of leaves and bushes became the sound of voices. The voices became footsteps. The footsteps became people they could see. First, only movement between the trees. They got closer and Martin could make out individual bodies. Hundreds maybe more. But not as many as the Union men defending their wall. They outnumbered the Rebels, and they would hold their ground. Martin could tell just by looking at the difference in numbers. The only thing he had to do was survive.

Time slowed—it always did—but Martin would be ready when the fight came.

The Rebels drew closer. They planted their feet and pushed their way up the hill, rifles in hand. Martin aimed, and held. Rebel forward progress stopped, thirty yards down the hill. Still, Martin held. The Rebels aimed their muskets and rifles at the line of Union soldiers above them. Still, Martin held his fire. Rebel gunfire erupted on the hillside, smoke clouding his line of sight. Still, Martin held. Through the fog of war, the rebels appeared, moving forward once again. Martin held a few more seconds while the rebel line cleared the smoke. With his vision clear, he fired his weapon, those on either side of him did the same. Most of the rebel line fell. Those that didn't, stood, stared then turned back.

"Be ready for another wave," a muted voice called from behind through the ringing in Martin's ears. "Check those next to you and report."

Before Martin could move, the man to his left grabbed his arm.

"You okay, Decay?" the man asked. Martin nodded.

He turned toward John, expecting his to see his friend's smiling face next to him, ready to make some joke. John was there, looking at him, but his face was colorless.

"John?"

"Got my shot off," John said his voice weak, pained.

"Shit. Where is it?"

John groaned, leaned back as best he could and grimaced. The front of his uniform was wet, dark red and dripping over the leaves and dirt.

"Guess I was up too high."

Martin did his best to laugh at the joke as he rolled John over on his back. He pressed both hands against the wound, but the blood poured out of him and seeped between the fingers of his gloved hand, the pressure he applied doing nothing to help his friend. But it was the only thing he could think to do. He looked up. Others were doing the same to the few men hit during the assault.

"This is it, Martin. You know it is. Get those gloves off me and grab your damned rifle with them."

"No." Martin pressed harder, but knew his friend was right.

"Here comes another wave," Chambers voice boomed.

"Listen, John, there's something I need you to know." Martin put his head close to John's. He felt tears coming on, but it wasn't the time for tears or sadness. He held death in his hands, but death was also coming up the hill and there was no time for grief. He needed to focus on keeping himself alive. John would want that. But still, he leaned in close to John, whispered in his ear and told him why he wore the gloves. Before he could get the whole story out, John was gone.

Eyes dry, Martin reloaded his rifle and prepared for the next wave of Rebel attack. They held it off, and the next one as well. The Rebels made no more runs at them on that hill.

When the day was over, they began to treat the wounded and remove the bodies of the dead. It was then that Martin cried. The war was behind him for the moment and he allowed himself to feel. Martin didn't notice right away but eventually realized that most of the others, even people he was close with, kept their distance from him. At first, he thought they were giving him space after the loss of his friend, but it wasn't long before he determined the real reason they stayed away. The secret he'd whispered to John Baxter as he died must not have been a whisper because everyone around him knew why his name was Decay. So much for being normal.

7

"Mornin' Decay," Marshall Ford, another soldier in Martin's company, said. Both just waking up, preparing for the day's march. The air was cool, technically still spring, but summer was again on the approach. It would be Martin's last summer at war. His time with the army was coming to an end and he couldn't wait to get home. He'd seen too many people he was close to die in his short time fighting. John's death hit Martin hard. He couldn't sleep, couldn't eat, lost weight and was slowly becoming shunned by most of the men he fought beside. It was hard to fight alongside people you didn't trust as much as you used to.

Summer in the south was a different animal compared to summer in the north. In spite of everything he'd seen, there wasn't much worse than wearing gloves for an entire southern summer.

The secret Martin thought he'd told John at the moment of his death hadn't been so secret. He'd learned later that he'd yelled the secret loud enough for the men around them to hear what he was saying. In that instant, not only did he lose his closest friend, but the secret he'd worked to keep his entire life was public. Once a few of the men knew, everyone knew and with the nickname came whispers, and Martin noticed the looks and smirks from the other men at times. As it had been when he was growing up, Martin felt it best to withdraw. He was close to a few men, but the rest, he distanced himself from. Even ones that were not outright hostile to him were ones he'd rather stay away from. At the same time, the men wanted less and less to do with Martin.

Whenever they had down time, at night or in between marches, Martin was usually the topic of conversation. But not in the way he wished they'd talk about him. His ability should have made him feared, but instead it made them talk about him like he wasn't there. As time wore on, most of the discussion centered on how Martin could be turned into a weapon of war.

It made sense. Martin understood why they thought he'd be useful, but he still didn't like it. They didn't know his past, about his parents or Mary-Louise. They didn't know what it was like to live with an ability like his.

Marshall Ford was one of the men Martin trusted. He wasn't as close to Martin as John Baxter had been, but it wasn't that type of relationship.

"I appreciate the things you said last night, Ford. Most people wouldn't speak up," Martin said. He rubbed the side of his cheek, the long hair of his beard itching. He used to shave one a week but lately it had become once a month, if that.

"Ain't nothin'. I reckon I wouldn't like people talking about me that way, so I wanted to make sure I did the same for you." Ford started deconstructing the tent so they could pick it up and move it for the day's march. They were headed further east into Tennessee. The men were sore, tired, but the march was necessary to end to the war.

"I appreciate it. I'm just like everyone else, you know. Just got this—this thing. The way I effect things around me," Martin said, not comfortable talking about it.

Ford nodded, continuing packing the tent.

The march was long and the cool spring morning gave way to a hot spring day. Martin wished he could take his gloves off as the day wore on, sweat from his palms soaking the inside of the leather gloves. The leather was already cracked and worn from years of use and days of sweating, but some days they bothered him more than others. Other than the gloves Martin kept the same uniform as everyone else. It didn't matter as much because everyone knew what he was anyway. They could protect themselves like Gabe had back when they were kids. Still, the gloves were an extra insurance policy.

They marched in rows of two. Martin knew most of the men around him: Ford and George Anderson, William Ruff, James Wilson and a few others. They weren't all friends, but they were all close. Martin had to trust these men with his life and on more than one occasion and they trusted him with theirs. Long marches were good for one thing, getting to know the people you marched with, and Martin knew these men well. They'd seen friends die together, had seen one another at their lowest point.

Martin exhaled, using the sleeve of his coat to wipe the sweat from his face.

"You should take the gloves off, Decay. Just don't touch anything," George Anderson said. It was like he was reading his mind. Martin wanted to take them off, had been debating it for more than an hour.

They marched another mile, maybe more and Martin decided it was time. He'd not taken his gloves off his hands for more than a minute since before the war, but the heat and sweat, was too much.

He hadn't touched anything other than his rifle for hours. There was little chance he'd be presented with the need to touch a tree or shake hands with someone else. Meeting anyone of a higher rank required a salute, not a hand shake, and the men around him knew better than to touch his skin. Without slowing his march or putting down his weapon, Martin pulled off one glove, then the other and stuffed them both into his belt so they wouldn't fall.

The absence of gloves cooled him. It was still warm out, still sunny, the ever-present southern humidity making sure he wasn't comfortable, but the air on his moist palms was a drastic improvement over the thick, damp leather gloves. His hands could breathe and the sweat made the air feel downright cool.

"How is that? Better?" Anderson asked, a smile on his face. Martin said nothing, he could feel the relief written all over his face.

The sun lowered in the sky, the shadows of the men stretching out on their right and the days march should have been nearing an end. There'd been no word from the officers at the front end of the march, so Martin had no idea if there was a destination they were aiming for or if they were simply looking for a proper place to stop for the night. They'd been marching for almost two years. He'd grow accustomed to long days of nothing but walking, but still by the end of the day, Martin's feet couldn't take much more. He felt every step and every imperfection in his boots. They'd passed many free, open fields and grasslands on the trek through Tennessee, plenty of places to make camp for the night, but hadn't stopped. It told Martin that General Riggs had a specific destination in mind.

Darkness settled in and the march continued. They travelled two by two. The entire column of men was well over two miles long. Men on horseback rode up and down the line distributing torches at random intervals. It gave them just enough light to see where the next painful footstep would land. But they did not stop, did not slow down. Martin's feet ached and throbbed. This had become the longest march he'd been on in his tenure with the army. His legs were sore, they couldn't be pushing much further than this, his feet wouldn't last.

At least his hands were cool. He patted his waist to check for the gloves in his belt. They were there. And the march pressed on.

Chirping of crickets surrounded them along with the steady rhythm of boots against packed earth. Martin continued the steady pace. Around him most of the day was conversation, laughing, joking but after twelve hours, the conversation stopped. There was nothing to laugh or joke about, nothing new to discuss. The men only wanted to get off their feet.

"Halt," a voice called from somewhere in front of him. A few more steps and the march stopped. Heads craned to either side, looking for signs of camp being made. At first, Martin saw nothing. Then ahead and off to his right a group of the torches gathered. As he watched, the number of torches increased and spread out. With the increased light Martin made out the outline of white tents. They'd decided to set up camp.

8

WITH CAMP SET UP, the men sat by the fire, passed small portions of chicken and beans to eat, and a jug of rum to drink. Martin put his gloves back on and luckily, the discussion hadn't yet turned to him.

"Where do you think we are? Still in Tennessee?" George Anderson asked the twelve men sitting around the fire with them.

Silence.

Martin didn't know all of the others around the fire by name, but he recognized them all. George Anderson and Marshall Ford were there along with William Marcus Trieste and James Broad. The rest were men whose names he never got around to learning. It was a good group, people he'd spend time with if given a choice. Except for James Broad, who was the biggest proponent of his becoming an undercover spy and shaking hands with the Rebs whenever possible. But they were exhausted and it wasn't likely anyone was going to give him a hard-time about his special touch.

The silence continued and no one ever answered George's question, a few simply nodding while they chewed or drank. But no one spoke up. Either they didn't have an opinion as to their whereabouts or they didn't care. Martin included himself in the latter group.

Wherever they were, it was temporary and they'd be gone come morning. Why worry about it one way or the other?

Martin was tired but didn't feel like sleeping. After they'd all eaten something, most of the men went back to their tents leaving Martin, Marshall Ford and one of the men whose name escaped him.

"Tell me something, Marcus," the man whose name he didn't know said. "I'm not saying this to be like some of these others, you're human just like the rest of us. But in all seriousness, every time we've been in a skirmish, we've killed people. We shoot them, they die. Our people die too."

Martin nodded. The guy was talking to him, but didn't know his name. At least the ignorance went both ways. Martin didn't bother to correct him about his name. He knew where the conversation was headed and didn't much care to get to know this man any more. Martin had become something of a celebrity, even though not everyone knew his name. The man's large moustache stretched from the middle of one cheek, to the middle of the other. The uneven light thrown off by the fire made it hard to see his features clearly. Marshall lit up a cigar next to Martin and the man continued.

"So, what I'm saying is: if you can kill someone with a rifle or bayonet why not kill them with...you know, with the ability that you have there."

Same question just worded differently. At least whoever this was had listened to his replies about killing people before. Marshall puffed out some cigar smoke and offered one to Martin; he declined.

"James." Marshall held out a cigar to their companion and he took it, nodding. James Harrison, *that* was the man's name. Martin silently thanked Marshall and then decided to respond as James lit his cigar.

"I guess I understand why you think that way, James," Martin said. "Though it's much more difficult when you actually have this *ability* as you call it. There is a lot of responsibility that comes with it. I don't think, and I've never thought this way, war or no war, that you should stab someone else in the back. If I'm going to fight you, or kill you, I think it's only fair that you should know it's coming and have a chance to defend yourself. Sneaking in, shaking hands and waiting for them all to die, is not an honorable way to fight a war. I don't want to fight that kind of war."

James tilted his head back and blew a steady cloud of smoke up into the air over his head. He sucked on the cigar again and tilted his head as if contemplating what Martin just told him. Then he blew the smoke out again. Marshall broke the silence.

"Martin shared that with me before. And it makes sense to me. We know when we're in a fight. They have a right to know too."

"I understand that, but do we really believe there are rules in war? Because I think this whole discussion comes down to your philosophy on that," James said.

Martin laughed. "We sound like a bunch of officers right now sitting around and philosophizing about war."

The other men laughed as well. They sat and listened to the fire crackle and the crickets chirp and sing.

"I appreciate you talking to me like that," Martin said. "I don't get close with many people out here lately because they all look at me as a weapon and nothing more. Treat me that way too. We don't talk much, but you don't treat me the way the others do."

"Ain't nothing," James said. "We all have to fight on the same side. Best to treat the men who watch your back the way you'd want to be treated. Some of them others just want to bully you into doing it, but you're right. They don't know what it's like. I don't know either. No one knows really 'cept you. So, whatever you believe, I gotta believe that's the way we should go too. I guess you could say you're the expert. Riggs and Chambers, they're the experts at fighting war and we listen to them, trust them and take their orders. But you're the expert of...you know, of that. And I think we should all trust you and listen to your thoughts of that."

"I'll drink to that," Marshall said. He held up the bottle of rum, which had to be nearly empty. He raised the bottle to his lips and took a sip, then passed it to Martin who took the bottle in a gloved hand and had his own sip, the brown liquid warmed his throat and his stomach. Then he passed the bottle to James who tipped the bottle far back and drained the rest in his mouth.

Silence returned between them. There was nothing more to say. Most of the fires were shrinking, soon to burn themselves out. Their own fire was smaller than it had been when the others were here eating, if they were going to continue to use it for light, they'd have to add more wood. But none of the men moved to get more. Martin guessed not many of the men were still awake. It would be an early morning and possibly another twelve or fourteen hour march across unknown land. It was time to get some sleep.

"I'm going to turn in, gentlemen," Martin said as he stood up, his muscles tight and back aching. That constant state of pain had become normal since the war started. The combination of long consecutive days of marching and sleeping on hard-packed dirt and grass every night made him permanently sore. If there was one thing he missed most in his time at war, it was his bed.

He left the two men while they finished their cigars, got as comfortable as he could inside his tent and fell asleep as soon as his body lay flat on the ground.

9

THE SOUND of a bugle call before sunrise did not surprise him. What did surprise him was the tune. It was not the call to rank he'd been expecting, which would have signaled another day's march. It was instead the call to camp tune, alerting the men that they would be here at camp another day. There would be no marching, but it didn't mean there wasn't work to do. He'd be busy all day. But a day of rest after the marathon march the day before would be welcomed by all the men.

Martin rolled over and put his hands on his face. He rubbed his eyes with his bare hands. At first, what was happening didn't register in his head, he was still half asleep after a late night and a few mouthfuls of rum, but the longer his hands stayed on his face the more he realized the problem.

His gloves were gone.

Martin sat up, the bleariness gone from his vison, the fuzzy feeling that followed sleep gone as well. Replacing it was worry, fear, anger. He got on his knees inside the tent and looked every-where, wondering if he'd pulled off the gloves accidentally while he slept. They were nowhere. He'd been wearing them his entire life; he wouldn't just pull them off. Still, he gave his fellow soldiers the benefit of the doubt. Maybe they came off or he dropped them. He stepped out of the tent and searched around the perimeter. Still no gloves.

He had no recollection of taking them off while he slept, no memory of someone coming in and taking them off his hands either. But something told him they were gone because someone wanted them gone. Someone pulled them off his hands and he needed to find out who it was.

Days at camp were drastically different from marching days. Although they worked hard, the food was more plentiful and the men got three large meals instead of just the singular big meal at the end of a long day of marching. They were given more breaks as well. This day was no different. Martin picked up a bowl of warm grits with an ungloved hand and sat to eat. He paid close attention to those passing him, watching for someone looking at him more closely than usual. He felt paranoid, but also as though the circumstances warranted a bit of paranoia on his part.

Of the men who walked by, no one mentioned his hands being free from his gloves until Marshall came and sat down next to him, his own bowl of warm grits cradled in his hands.

"Mornin' Martin," he said. He didn't turn his head toward Martin, just sat, hunched over his bowl in much the same way Martin hunched over his own. But even without looking at him, Marshall was observant. "What happened to your gloves?"

If it had been anyone else asking, Martin would have suspected them, but he trusted Marshall. He wouldn't have expected John Baxter to take his gloves without telling him, and John didn't even know why he wore the gloves. In much the same way, Martin didn't think Marshall was the one who stole his gloves. There were a few constants in the world, and Martin knew he could trust Marshall.

"They weren't on my hands when I woke up. Not in my tent or around it either. And I know I had them when I went to sleep last night. Trust me, I'd never take them off in my sleep. Someone took 'em." Martin shook his head and his lips pressed together. He had to stop thinking about it because his anger grew.

"I'd say so, Martin." Marshall shifted on the log they sat on, moved closer to Martin. "Maybe I should have told you this earlier. I'm sorry I didn't. There is a movement to get you working as a spy, like they all want you to do. Supposedly, it's coming from high up. They know about you Martin. Colonel Chambers you probably already suspected, but Generals too. Hell, maybe even Lincoln himself heard the stories about Decay. Word is they have a plan for you. Want you to start killing Rebs from up close. Send you behind enemy lines. Meet them, take them out. Maybe even get close to Johnston or Lee or someone like that. Shake their hands, they get sick and die or however it works, war is over. *They* want you to do that, not just the people here. The decision makers. If someone took your gloves, it was on orders I bet." Then after a long pause: "Sorry I didn't tell you earlier."

"They all know about it? About what happens?" Martin asked staring at his hands.

"Well, you know, no one really knows what happens. Coupla' us heard the stories you've told. From there I think word spread but no one really knows," Marshall said. Martin nodded and Marshall continued. "One of the officers heard a few of the men talking about it, talking about the nickname too. I was just standing there listening, but when the officer came by, he said he was passing the word up the chain. Then ordered them and me not to say anything to you. Threatened torture if we told you so—well—I've been debating telling you anyway the last couple days. Then when I saw you with no gloves on, I figured something might have happened." His speech was low and he kept looking over his shoulder and around him while he talked. There were others around but no one close enough to hear what he was saying.

"I appreciate it," Martin said, still unsure of what to do with the information he'd been given. "You're taking a chance telling me, then."

"Anyone asked, you didn't hear all this from me."

Martin nodded and Marshall kept his head down, stood up and walked away.

He sat on the log a while longer, bowl empty. They'd always asked him why he didn't use his ability to end the war, and he'd always given them the same answer. They didn't have to know about his past. He'd never shared that with anyone. He wanted more than anything to just be a normal soldier. He had been until his secret got out. His vow was with himself and no one else. He didn't think he had to share it, but maybe it was the only way to get all of these people of his back about it. He thought the answer he'd been giving was the right one. The answer that he thought everyone would want him to give. The honorable answer. An answer he could be proud of. And the answer God Himself would want. But almost every person who knew about him thought he should do the opposite. Now he'd learned people he looked up to, people he admired, thought he should go ahead and use his ability to end this war. Maybe he needed to give them more. Maybe they needed more than just the answer he'd rehearsed in his head since the day John died. Actions sometimes spoke louder than words ever could and if there was one thing Martin could do with his ability it was take action.

If he still had John, he'd go talk to his friend, explain what was happening and hope they could work out a solution together. John wasn't there, and Marshall was a friend, but not the way John Baxter had been. He didn't have anyone to go to with this kind of problem, so he had no choice but to take action.

In the middle of the open field where the tents were set up was a large, leafy tree. The branches reached up high and its tremendous width meant when the sun was at its zenith, it would provide a lot of shade during the midday break to eat. It was under the tree where most of the men gathered, even though the sun was not yet high in the sky. The shade of the tree would provide a great place to sit and rest while they ate, away from the burning rays of hot sun they were to be subjected to the rest of the day.

Martin got up, weaved his way through the men standing or sitting on the grass eating their grits. On one side of the tree stood a table with the empty used bowls stacked up in a tower—one inside the next—almost as tall as Martin. He went to the table, added his bowl to the top of the tower then turned away from the table. It was a purposeful turn and it left him facing the trunk of the tree. Martin gave a quick glance up at its height and the leaves that hung from its branches. He took caution not to linger and draw attention. Then he reached out and placed his palm against the trunk of the tree. It was rough and felt cool to the touch, even as the air warmed around him. Martin concealed a smile, being able to touch nature again, its most raw form, felt good, comforting. He didn't want to stay longer than necessary so he reluctantly pulled his hand away and turned away from the tree and left the area.

Martin formed up with his company to get his orders for the day. While receiving orders, they found out the real reason they had stopped. The Rebel Army was about two days in front of them and headed west, right for them. Union scouts located them the day before and rode like hellfire to get back and announce their approach. The news made him look at the ground they found themselves on differently. It wasn't just a place to stop, but a future battlefield. Martin wasn't an officer, but had been in enough engagements to know what good ground looked like. To their north, thick woods. To the south and west it was flat, with few fences, the road they marched in on was the only easy transportation route. To their east, the direction the Rebel Army would approach from, gently rolling hills, the highest of which they were already on top of. They were to spend the next few days fortifying their position and preparing for the inevitable clash with the opposing army. At least they held the high ground.

By mid-morning the green leaves on the large tree had all changed color. The tree belonged in Massachusetts in the middle of October, not Tennessee in late spring. Martin continued his work but kept one eye on the tree. By the lunch break, the branches of the massive tree were bare, leaves covered the tables, tents and food underneath it like a blanket. Martin had a hard time keeping the grin off his face as the men rustled through the leaves to pick up their lunches. The few men who didn't know Martin or his ability looked at the tree in wonder, no doubt trying to figure out how the tree could lose so many leaves in just a few hours. The ones that did know, glared at him.

"Quigley," a voice bellowed from behind him as Martin took his bowl of soup. He held the bowl and turned to face Colonel Chambers.

"Sir." Martin stood and saluted, bowl of soup his free, ungloved hand.

"Quigley, the damn General is not happy with you. I think we know what this is about." Chambers eyed the dying tree. "That's not good for either of us. Now we both need to go see him. Put the soup down and let's go."

Martin was starving, but followed orders. He'd made it a point to work harder than anyone else all morning. If he was going to get called out, he didn't want it to be for not working his share so he pushed himself to work harder than the others. Same with the soup. He knew everyone would know he'd messed with the tree, but in every other aspect of his day he needed to be perfect, so he put his soup down in spite of his hunger.

They weaved across camp, through the other men. They passed close by so Martin kept his arms crossed, hands tucked under his armpits as they maneuvered their way to the other side of the field, past the soldier's tents to the largest tent. General James Riggs was inside. Martin had only ever seen the man from a distance and never spoken to him. The General was only two people removed from President Lincoln and corresponded with him on a regular basis. According to Marshall, General Riggs and the other commanders knew all about his ability. It was no wonder he was getting called in after what happened with the tree. As they approached the entrance to the tent, there was a loud crack behind them. If he hadn't been expecting it, Martin would have thought it was a gunshot, but he turned just in time to see a branch from the tree crash to the ground below.

"Oh, hell," Chambers said. "Let's go."

Chambers turned and entered the tent, Martin followed.

Standing at a table with a map of the area spread out was

General Riggs. Martin was surprised at how young the man seemed. He wasn't sure about his age, but the idea of a general in his mind was someone much older than him. This man appeared to be in his thirties, at most. His wide moustache went almost from ear to ear and the small patch of hair on his chin hung down and covered his neck, but there was nary a grey hair. Regardless of his age, Riggs had the look of a general, that much was certain.

"Sir," Chambers said, standing at attention and saluting. Martin did the same.

"At ease, men," Riggs said, then looked at Martin. "Chambers, you can leave us." He never took his eyes off Martin. Chambers gave a quick nod then turned and left the tent.

"Have a seat Mr. Quigley," Riggs motioned to one of the two chairs at the edge of the tent. The shade the tent provided was a break from the sun, but the lack of airflow kept it warm inside. The chair was right next to the wall of the tent and air vented in from outside. It provided some coolness. Martin sat, the General sitting opposite him. "Your name is Martin, right?"

"Yes, Sir," Martin replied. His back straight, not even touching the back of the chair. He felt stiff and probably looked stiffer than he felt.

"Martin, from now until the time we stand up from these chairs, we are not soldiers. We are two men fighting the same fight. Friends. You relax, and call me James. I'll call you Martin. When we stand up, we're soldiers again and you'll go back to calling me Sir."

"Yes, Si—," Martin started and then stopped himself. He just nodded instead.

"Alright, so tell me what do you think of this war, Martin." Riggs leaned back in his chair, reaching into the front pocket of his uniform and pulling out a cigar. It was long and he didn't have a match in his hand so he just spun the cigar against his palm, smelling it a few times.

"I'm not sure what you mean?"

"The war. I know some men can't figure out why we're fighting just to free the damn slaves. Doesn't make sense to them. They trust the President, they love Massachusetts or New Jersey or wherever they're from, so they fight. But they don't necessarily agree with it. Just wondering where you stand on that."

Martin took in a long breath. He knew where he stood on the issue, but wasn't sure where the General stood and, more importantly, wasn't sure the point of the conversation. Even though the General said they were just talking, there were still right and wrong answers in all of this. The conversation still had a point.

"Well, I actually think it's a great thing we are doing. It might not be the reason a lot of men are fighting, but freeing the slaves makes sense to me. President wants it done, it's probably the right thing to do. Slavery, it just doesn't make sense to me. They're different than us, sure, but that doesn't mean we should own 'em."

Riggs nodded, spun his cigar between his fingers again, smelled the end.

"Lots of men would be nervous to say that kind of thing. No one's really sure where anyone else stands. Especially those of us higher in rank. I happen to believe the same thing you do. And I believe in Abraham Lincoln. I'll do what he says because I think it's the right thing to do, because I trust him, and I love this country."

Martin nodded, waiting for Riggs to get to the point.

"Reason I ask," Riggs went on, leaning forward, looking Martin in the eyes, "is that we need to trust each other and trust what our superior officers say and what they order us to do. I don't command the entire army and I don't take orders directly from Lincoln. There's an extra layer in there so, just like you, I follow orders."

"Yes," Martin said, resisting the urge to follow it up with the word 'sir.' "I agree. We have to follow orders or there wouldn't even be an army. And to be honest I'd say I'm one of the most loyal and honest soldiers out there. There've been people who've told me things they've done that go against direct orders that I couldn't believe. A lot of them are gone, but some of them are not."

He knew saying something like that to a superior was asking for trouble, but the men in his company caused him enough trouble, he could give it back to them a different way. If Riggs wanted names, Martin would give them.

"Indeed, so I've heard. *That* is the particular reason we are sitting here right now instead of me standing over there." Riggs nodded his head back toward the entrance to the tent where'd they'd stood a minute before. "If I didn't think you were one of the good ones, we wouldn't be doing this. And everything you've said so far, lets me know I made the right decision."

The breeze gusted outside, the walls of the tent flapping back and forth. Another loud crack, then a crash from outside was followed by the groans and yells of men. Riggs either didn't hear it or didn't want to acknowledge it. Martin decided he liked him; he didn't get the sense that Riggs was just saying what Martin wanted to hear. He truly believed everything he was saying. It made Martin trust him.

"So now that we're sitting here as friends," Riggs continued, "let me tell you that I've heard about the effect you can have on living things. Do you care to tell me about it?"

Martin exhaled hard through his nose. This was what he was expecting. Riggs was just going about it differently. It was always going to come back to his ability.

"Not much to tell, really. I don't know why it happens or exactly how it works. But I've had it almost all my life. I touch things, they die. That's about the long and short of it."

"So, people, animals, plants..." he looked in the direction of the entrance to the tent, paused and smiled, "...trees, anything alive?"

"Yes," Martin replied.

"How did you learn you had this ability?"

"I'd rather not discuss it, if that's ok." Martin felt his face flush. He didn't want to have to go through the whole thing. He wouldn't tell the story no matter what.

"Sure. Of course. We're just friends here anyway."

"Thank you," Martin exhaled glad he didn't have to defend his decision not to share the events from his past.

"Why would you not tell the army about this ability of yours then?" Riggs tucked the cigar back in his coat pocket and steepled his fingers.

"Still friends?" Martin asked.

Riggs nodded. "We're still sitting here."

"In that case, I'm not sure why it's the army's business to know that about me. I keep to myself, do what I'm told, more than the average soldier. What business is it of the army if this thing is a part of me? Always will be. Doesn't change who I am. I always came as just a normal soldier, no different from anyone else."

"Let's put that aside for now." Riggs leaned back again and Martin could tell he wanted to get up out of the chair, but didn't. "Tell me about the tree today."

"Still sitting?" Martin asked.

Riggs spun the cigar, nodded.

"I wear gloves. To keep from touching someone or something by accident. It's the only way I can make sure I keep this ability under control. I grew up trying to keep it hidden and also trying not to hurt anyone. The gloves have worked for me since I was about six." Martin stopped, realizing he was headed down the wrong path and refocused his description elsewhere. "Anyway, someone who obviously knows about me, took my gloves while I was sleeping last night. When I got breakfast this morning, I must have touched the tree, you know absentmindedly, something that happens all the time and you don't even notice you do it. I don't have that luxury. Without my gloves I have to keep track of every little detail. And well, you can see why I keep the gloves on."

"It happens that fast?"

"Well I guess the thing—whatever I touch—starts dying the moment I touch it, that's always been my guess. The tree isn't dead yet, but it's dying. By tomorrow morning it will be completely dead."

"And this happened because someone stole your gloves?" Riggs leaned forward again.

Martin nodded and looked at Riggs.

"It's time to stand up, Martin.," Riggs stood up first.

"Yes, Sir," Martin said, standing.

"Mr. Quigley, I ordered your gloves to be taken last night." He walked to a table in the corner of the tent and pulled open the drawer as he talked. "We'd heard the rumors, but according to the story no one has actually seen this ability of yours in action. We didn't know if it was just a rumor or the truth so I wanted to find out without confronting you. You're a good soldier. I'm sorry to do that to you the way we did."

Martin nodded, a surge of anger rushing through him. He knew what Marshall told him, but part of him assumed it wasn't true. Now he knew it was true. They'd taken advantage of him. For the first time in his life he wanted to use his ability to purposely take a life. He wanted to reach out and touch the General's hand. If Riggs wanted to see how it worked, Martin could show him.

But he didn't.

He restrained himself.

"Mr. Quigley, there is no easy way to say this. I want you to become a spy for us. Infiltrate the Rebel Army and kill them in a way only you can. I understand not wanting to do that because you're just being a normal soldier like everyone else. The problem is you're not like everyone else. You're different and we have to treat you different. You're a weapon and you can save so many lives."

"Sir," Martin started, but Riggs kept going before he could get more words out.

"I understand. Think about it this way though, Quigley. The men you kill—they are probably going to die in battle anyway. It's not about the Rebel lives you'll be saving. It's Union lives. Our lives. For every piece of lead we send across a field, one comes back at us. Every engagement, almost as many of our men die as theirs. You've seen it firsthand. You lost a close friend Chambers told me. Baxter. Damn all the military school stuff about high ground and army position. I learned it in a classroom. You lived it. You know all about that. You know that even if we win the engagement and they retreat, there are bodies left on both sides. Someone like you, someone who can kill with a touch, can save their lives." Riggs pointed in the direction of the men outside the tent. "Come this way."

Riggs put an arm around Martins shoulder and guided him through the opening of the tent and out into the sunlight and the heat. Chambers still stood there waiting for them. Riggs regarded the Colonel only long enough to give the man a curt nod.

"Chambers, we are going to need some privacy again," Riggs said.

Martin saw his direct commanding officer's face drop as he was dismissed for a second time. Martin stifled a smile.

"Look at them, Mr. Quigley," Riggs pointed at the mass of humanity on the field preparing for battle. "I'm sure there are people there you don't like. I know there's people there I don't like. But they are our people and there are people I *do* like out there too. Do you want them to die? Because this battle, tomorrow or the next day, half of them, maybe more, will be gone. That includes me and it includes you. It included John Baxter. Not saying you could have stopped that, but there are other John Baxters here, Martin. It's my job, *our* job, to protect them."

Martin shook his head. Could Martin have stopped his death? He didn't think so, but now Riggs had put the thought in his mind. It was possible.

There was a long silence, Riggs' words hanging in the air, Martin's mind racing. It was awkward and Martin felt like he should say something, tell Riggs about John and how he died, fill Riggs in about how it came to be that everyone knew about Martin's special ability. But he didn't, instead keeping his mouth shut. Martin understood what Riggs was trying to do. He was doing a better job of convincing him to use his ability than anyone else ever had. But Martin was angry. Riggs, and whoever helped him, treated him like a thing. A weapon. A tool. Anything but normal.

"I could order you to do this, Martin. And you're a good soldier, so you'd probably do it. But I want you to *want* to do it. It would make you a hero. It would save lives and it could end the war."

Anger ripped him apart. Martin rocked back and forth on his

feet; it was good they were standing because he couldn't sit still. He was ready to reach out and touch Riggs, wrap an ungloved hand around his throat, then stay with him, hear the coughs, watch him die.

He was a good person. He could never do that. He had power. A power that made him different. He couldn't let momentary rage get the best of him. Martin took a long breath in and clasped his hands together to keep from trembling.

"Sir," he said, calm, relaxed, conflicted, "I understand. Believe me when I say I think about it every day."

"I've told the other men a similar thing before. I guess I can repeat it here. Because I do understand the point of view that makes me a weapon. How easy it would be to debilitate their army with me around them. But when we fight, we fight face to face. The Rebs come at us, they know they are facing death and come anyway. We do the same thing. If—if I did what you all are asking, they wouldn't know there was a fight. Wouldn't even see it coming until it was too late. That, in my mind, is not an honorable way to fight, Sir."

"I can understand that, Mr. Quigley, and I respect that. You're the exact kind of person we need in this situation, because you respect the power you have. I don't think you will take advantage of it. But what we need to finish this war is someone unique. Someone who can take lives quietly. The war isn't going to end without someone like that. We can find others. Spies. Assassins. Call them what you want. They can go in and do it. Assassinate silently, retreat and repeat. Or we can give them you."

Another silence. Martin knew what he was going to say and it made him angry. But he had no choice.

"Alright, Sir," he said, jaw clenched tight, "I'll do it."

10

RIGGS WAS PREPARED. He knew Martin would say yes. He didn't go back to his tent to rejoin the men. Once he'd agreed, Riggs shuffled him back into the tent. He had clothes—southern looking clothes—and a story to tell the Rebs when he saw them. Martin got his instructions: take out some of the rebels to make sure there was no attack, demoralize them. And if he could, get close to General Montgomery and some of his lieutenants and take them out too. When Martin returned to camp in a week or two, it would be easy to take the land from the retreating Confederates and continue their march, probably without a fight. He got an extra helping of lunch and was pushed out of camp, headed east, prepared to meet up with the enemy before they marched west and the battle began.

Martin was on his own. The sun was lower in the sky but the heat and humidity ever-present. And then there were the nerves. He was from Massachusetts, a Union soldier marching right into the face of the Confederate Army.

He had a plan and a story, one drawn up by the highest members of the Union military, maybe even with input from Lincoln himself. It was possible Lincoln knew his name.

It was all riding on his accent. He'd practiced with Riggs who determined Martin's approximation of southern English adequate enough to proceed. But would Riggs have said no if it wasn't good enough? Or just sent him anyway? He'd never know. He went over his speech aloud to himself as he walked, speaking in his fake 'suthen' accent to practice as much as possible before the show started.

He knew the Confederates were out there. They were close, so he kept his voice low, his eyes open.

At dusk, he saw them. Three armed men along the side of the road, sentries meant to protect the exact location of the army and its generals.

"Hold there," one of the men said.

Martin stopped. "Lord, thank goodness I found ya," he said, keeping his southern accent but trying his best not to overdo it.

"Who are you?" Another of the sentries asked.

"Charles Weston here, Sir. I— I's taken pris'ner by the Yanks back in Kentucky. They been forcin' me to march with 'em since." Martin lifted his feet and showed the men his tattered boots, soles completely worn off to his bare feet in places. "They knew you was out here 'n stopped paying attention to me. Kept hearin' 'em say you was close by. So, when I had the chance, I ran off. I reckon I'd find you if I came this way and thank the lord you're here."

The sentries looked at each other. It was clear Martin was unarmed and he was in Confederate clothes and worn shoes. He looked the part and had an actual name to give them of an actual person, dead in Kentucky.

The first one who spoke gave a nod, the others doing the same. They bought it.

"Thank you, thank you. I'm so glad I found ya'll." Martin said then extended an uncovered hand.

He shook hands with all three of the sentries. He'd never purposefully used his ability like that before. With Mary-Louise it was an unfortunate side effect he didn't want. It had always been something he tried to control, to contain. He'd never let it become unleashed like this before. This was the first time he used his power with the sole intention of taking a person's life. These men would be the first of many over the next twenty-four hours to decay and die because of his actions.

One of the sentries led him down a path he could barely see. As the woods around them thickened, light worked its way through the trees and the outskirts of the rebel camp between the leaves and brush.

"Just up here," the man said. Martin still didn't know his name.

"Well hidden back her., Yanks would never have found us," Martin said.

"No, Sir. That's the hope. From what you said, I guess they already saw us though. General Montgomery will want to see you. We'll go to him then he'll probably want to set you up in a division, get you a weapon."

Martin nodded. General Montgomery, the sentry, and as many others as he could get close to, would be dead, or close to it, by noon the next day.

He was brought to a large tent, not unlike the tent of General Riggs back at Union camp.

"Wait here," the sentry said, then disappeared inside. There were muffled voices but Martin couldn't make out anything being said. Then silence, the sentry stuck his head out the flap. "General will see you."

Martin went in the tent and went through the story he'd gone over with Riggs, even going so far as to mention General Heth who would have been his commanding general in Kentucky if he'd actually fought there. The General didn't seem skeptical and bought the story pretty much as Martin told it. He had yet to offer to shake hands, Martin didn't want to push. He felt a twinge of nervous anxiety as he waited for the moment Montgomery put out his hand, though it wasn't a given that he'd get the chance. He could only hope that the man would and if he didn't, Martin could still decimate the army, he just needed the opportunity.

"We'll lick 'em, and we need more men like you, Mr. Weston. Escaped prisoner, right back on the line," Montgomery said with his thick southern drawl. Montgomery patted Martin's shoulder and moved in close to him.

"Thank you, Sir," Martin saluted, nodded. Then, finally, when Montgomery extended his hand, and Martin shook it. That tingling sensation—the one he'd become so used to that he barely noticed it anymore—was there and stronger than ever. In that moment, with the General's hand wrapped around his own, Martin understood why people had been after him to use the ability for so long. He never really understood until then. He'd grown up with the ability, lived with it and respected it. This was different. In the handshake, Martin saw the end of the war. He saw his mark on history. He saw how he could *change* history. He was more powerful than General Montgomery. The handshake proved that. He was more powerful than Riggs. More powerful than any General. More powerful even, than Lincoln or Davis. He was the most powerful force in the war. He just never realized it before.

They finished their handshake and Martin smiled. "Always glad to help the Confederacy," he said.

"Indeed." Montgomery returned the smile. "Mr. Cook will take you to your new company," Montgomery said as he opened the flap to the outside. Cook, the sentry, must have overheard because he nodded and held his hand out motioning Martin to follow him.

Following another salute to their commanding officer, Martin and Cook left the tent. They were only a few steps away when Cook coughed. Martin smiled.

Decay had started.

11

MARTIN MET MOST of the men in his company. He shook their hands. They were not setting out to attack the Union Army the next day, which was perfect because by early afternoon he expected none of these men to be fit for walking. With each hand he shook, he felt more powerful and his thoughts on the matter began to change. Before long, he had an idea of what might be in store for more than just the men in his new company. He tried his best to keep track of the men whose hands he'd shook, but if things went right, it wouldn't matter.

Just as the Union soldiers spent the day making camp and preparing for defense, the Confederates had readied themselves for attack and they were exhausted. Before long, the men began turning in for the night. Coughing had increased. Martin noticed it, but wondered if anyone else had noticed as well. He should have been tired. Martin had worked for both sides of the war in the span of a few hours, but he was too excited. The power rushing through his body made him unable to rest or sleep or do anything other than wait for camp to turn in for the night.

Martin pretended to settle in too. He'd had a taste of the power he controlled and now he was ready to use it on a larger scale. But first he had to wait.

If this was anything like the Union camps, which he expected, there would be guards taking shifts on the outskirts of camp, but no one watching the interior. It would be dark and Martin would be able to do what he wanted.

Men went to sleep and Martin waited. There were coughs of the men around him, but they were all in their tents, sleeping, or trying to and beyond the circle of men around him, thousands more men he hadn't made contact with, yet.

The night grew darker, silent and desolate, soon to be devoid of life. And Martin waited. When there was no movement, no voices, only the sounds of coughs, Martin slipped from his tent. It was hot and most of the tents were open to let the cool breeze in. Even better for Martin. He slipped into a nearby tent. A man he hadn't seen before slept soundlessly on the ground. Martin lightly touched the exposed skin of the man's ankle. Then he moved to another tent —an exposed hand—Martin touched the back of it. He moved to yet another tent, and another, feeling the power grow in him with each Confederate soldier he touched. Darkness hid him when someone moved or woke up after the touch but Martin maintained his silence. A virus moving through camp, infecting the whole Confederate Army one man at a time.

He tried to keep count, but somewhere after two hundred, he lost track. He was more powerful than he'd felt his entire life. He wanted to get them all. There was still lots of night left. It only took a second to touch an ankle or a forehead or an arm, and so many seconds of darkness left. So many lives left.

The number of men coughing increased, as did the volume, but no one was out of their tents yet. The coughs should have affected Martin. They should have reminded him of his mother, his father, Mary-Louise, and they did. But the feeling was only one of anger. He'd been forced to live with this for an entire life. He'd hid it, felt it was his curse. Now, finally, after fighting against it for so long, he was able to use his ability for something good. This army would decay and die, and the war would end.

Some didn't sleep in tents, rather sleeping on top of blankets or even just flat on the grass. But Martin didn't care. He moved through them, the touch of decay spreading. The sky began to brighten, the dark, black sky becoming purple, then deep blue and Decay stopped touching the men.

Martin made his way back to his tent. He laid down, closed his eyes, pretended to be asleep and smiled at the coughing that surrounded him.

He was jolted awake by a bugle call similar to the one he'd heard the morning before when he was still with the Federal Army. For a moment he thought it had been a dream, but when he opened his eyes and heard the hacking coughs of the men around him, he remembered where he was. The sky didn't look that much brighter than when he fallen asleep. He guessed no more than a few minutes had passed. Martin smiled to himself and left his tent to look at the mass of decaying soldiers beginning their final day.

He'd done more damage than he originally planned. But once he started, he couldn't stop. He did manage to skip a few of the prone bodies here and there so he wouldn't be the only person not getting sick. Most of the army would be dead by the next morning and incapacitated well before then. It would be an incredible thing to watch.

The men lined up to get food and Martin joined them. They looked weak. Coughing was still intermittent with individuals, but it was hard to ignore in a large group because everyone was coughing. They took their food in bowls much like the Union soldiers did, except this was just broth, lukewarm. Martin stood and drank the broth down then returned his bowl which was refilled for someone else.

He examined them, looking for signs of death, signs of decay other than the coughs. He'd never watched someone die from his touch, only ever heard the coughs. It was coming. The sentries he shook hands with the day before and perhaps even General Montgomery were well on their way to death. But the men that surrounded him had only just started their journey.

Some of them he'd touched almost five or six hours ago, others less than an hour.

Martin's company formed up and he joined them. Many of them did not look well, but he was surprised they were still on their feet moving around. They were inventorying weapons then working to fix two cannons that had been spiked by the Yanks during a previous engagement. Weapons in the Confederacy were hard to come by and Montgomery hoped they could make something out of the damaged ones.

"Did you hear about Montgomery?" the soldier working with Martin asked between the coughs. Martin refused to remember his name.

Martin shook his head. "No, what happened? Did he get injured?"

"No one knows. Supposedly he's in bed, laid up for the day at least."

Martin shook his head, taking care to let his mouth downturn. "Not good news with the Federal Army as close as they are."

"They are really that close?" the man said. Martin saw the worry in his face. He needn't worry; he'd never see the Federal Army.

"Sure are," Martin said, then paused to let out a cough just to play along with everyone else. "I left them midday yesterday and found the sentries before sunset. Just down that road a-ways. They're not hiding neither. Got the high ground just waitin' for us to come marching up the road. They won't know what hit 'em though. We can take them."

The man nodded, coughed and went back to work.

By midday the coughing was widespread. The sentries were probably dead, General Montgomery too, depending on how healthy he was prior to their handshake.

Soon the whole field began to cough. Not just short quick coughs, but long coughing fits, three, and then five, then ten, and then fifteen men. All at the same time, doubled over coughing, unable to stop. And when they finally did, ten, fifteen, twenty more took their place. It was impossible not to realize something was wrong. Martin gave himself a coughing fit so no one noticed him. The men regained their composure after their fits and continued working. So did Martin.

"Must be something going around," someone nearby said.

"Maybe it was the Federals," another suggested. The others laughed it off, only Martin knew how close he was to the truth.

"Separate!" A voice shouted from the direction of the command tents. "Go back to your tents, your sleeping spots. Don't touch anyone! Wait for orders."

Martin turned and worked his way across the field to the tents. It was late afternoon but the sun was still up. His mission was almost over. He followed orders and returned to his tent. He talked to no one. Touched no one. Just sat, listened and, at times, coughed.

He laid down and before long, fell asleep to the sound of an entire camp coughing in the midst of its own decay.

He woke up to a quiet, still silence. The coughing, once deafening, was gone. The silence that took its place was calm, haunting. There would be no more coughing. Everyone lay in motionless stages of decay. A few of the men groaned, but most were silent.

He exited his tent and looked around. In the back, away from the mass of human meat that surrounded him, stood a small group of men. The ones he skipped. Martin looked around, acting surprised, then weaved in and around the tents and bodies of his debilitated enemies.

"What happened?" Martin asked when he got close to the rest of the living group. They stood in silence, staring at the dying men in front of them.

"No one knows," one of them said. "A plague or a virus or something."

"Seems like not all of us are affected," someone else said.

"Colonel Roberts is the highest rank still awake and alive. He sent two others to meet up with General Partson just north of here.

We were the largest group in the area. I don't think we will attack today."

Martin shook his head. "Maybe they're not all dead, just sick and they'll come out of it."

"Unlikely," the first man said. "Montgomery got sick yesterday. He died yesterday. Few others died too. They all had the exact same symptoms. Looks like some of us are immune but not many. This could wipe out millions. The next plague."

Martin ran a hand through his hair and turned his back to them to hide his smile.

"My God," Martin said, then let out a long breath. He turned back to face them, his face somber. "I think I need to take a walk and try to process all of this. I will meet you back here soon."

The men stood, saying nothing but nodding at him. Martin put out his hand. They each shook it and Martin walked away.

12

He planned on just walking out of the Confederate camp and returning to his Union brothers further down the road, but when he left the camp, he became less sure of himself.

He still had his gloves hidden in a pocket. He could feel them hit his leg with each step. Two days earlier, he'd not have gone anywhere without his gloves on. He'd have never taken them off. But after what he'd done. After seeing first-hand what he was capable of in just one night, he didn't want to wear the gloves anymore.

Martin veered off the path that would return him to camp. He needed time to sort through his thoughts and he couldn't do it with others around. They would have too much to say, too much input. This wasn't about them. Not anymore. It wasn't about the Federal Army, or General Riggs. Or Lincoln. It was about Martin Quigley. For the first time since his mother died, he no longer wanted to hide his ability. He shouldn't hide it. People wanted him to hide it because they were afraid. But Martin wasn't afraid of it anymore. He embraced it. He celebrated it. It was his ability—his *power*. He was the most powerful person on earth.

Martin tripped over a root sticking up out of the ground and careened deeper into the woods. He fell and hit his face against the hard-packed soil. He looked back at the root then reached out and wrapped his bare hand around it. He peered up at the tall tree attached to the root and smiled. He continued on a not-so-straight route through the woods, moving left and right, touching trees in his path, for no other reason than that he could. The world lived or died based on his touch—on his choice. He was stronger and more powerful that any general in the war, more powerful than Lincoln. He was a god and he could do anything. No one could stop him.

What would a god do in the face of war?

Everyone ought to be free and Martin believed in what the Union was trying to do. But was every soldier fighting and killing to free the slaves? Or did they not care about them one way or the other? Were they only interested in fighting? In killing? The latter was probably closer to the truth. There was one way to make sure the war ended. He wanted to save as many lives as he could and he knew how he could do it.

A smile grew on his face and he returned to the road that led to the Union camp.

Martin followed the road. He was a different man when he first followed this path toward the Confederate Army. Then, he'd been reluctant to use his ability as a weapon. He'd been the man who fought against it as much as possible. He wasn't that man anymore. The tents were in the same positions. Men still moved around, working, fortifying the Union position, a task Martin rendered unnecessary.

Decay smiled and walked back into camp.

A few men recognized him and greeted him. He smiled, nodded. Hands in his pockets, he walked toward General Riggs' tent. Martin moved to enter the tent, casually strolling past the guard in front. Before he could get inside, the guard stopped him. It was a different guard than the one there the previous day. Martin looked at him, the guard having no idea who he was. Martin wanted to put his hand on the man, teach him to respect those who were more powerful, but he didn't. The time wasn't right for such drastic action.

"I need to see the General," Martin said.

"The General is not seeing anyone at the moment,'" the reply came. Probably a standard answer for any request of such nature.

Martin didn't care.

"No, I'll see him now. Tell him it's Martin Quigley. He will see me." No more asking, Martin was telling people what to do from now on.

The guard stared at Martin, the anger in the man's face visible. The guard wouldn't kill Martin, so he had nothing to worry about. Martin stared back at him, not with anger in his heart or on his face; he looked at the man with total indifference. He didn't care one way or the other about the person in front of him. The stare lasted a few seconds longer than it should have. Martin moved to reach out and touch the guard, but the guard moved first.

"I'll tell him you're here," the guard said. He spun then entered the tent.

He was gone less than a minute before his head came through the slit in the white canvas. Martin's look had not changed. The guard was still angry.

"He says to come right in," the guard said. "Follow me."

Martin couldn't help but smile in the man's face. The guard ignored Martin's smile and led him into the tent. Riggs sat behind the desk, pretending to study the map in front of him, but Martin knew his only thoughts were on the outcome of Martin's mission

When the guard left, the General stood up. Martin saluted, though he hated it.

"Well, Mr. Quigley, I wasn't expecting you so soon. They didn't buy the story?"

"The mission is complete," Martin said. He normally would have followed that with the respectful 'sir,' but he didn't. It wasn't anything against Riggs personally. He liked the man, but didn't feel Riggs was better or deserved more respect than he did.

"Complete?" Riggs said. He paused and looked at Martin, eyes squinted. "Explain."

"You wanted me to stop them from attacking. I can guarantee none of them will be attacking."

"You demoralized them. Who died? Montgomery? The lieutenants? How do you know they are demoralized enough to not fight us? As we discussed, the plan was for you to be gone a week or two, reduce their numbers as a way to prevent an attack. The only way I'd know you completed your assignment was the fact that no attack came. Why are you here?"

Martin waited. He didn't say anything at first. Didn't move. Why would he attack strategically when he could do what he did? It didn't make sense in his mind.

"They're all dead. I killed them all. I spared a few so that they wouldn't question the fact that I was behind the deaths. But I shook their hands this morning before I left."

"You killed them all?" Riggs stared, his mouth hanging open. At first, Martin was angry that the man who changed him into a human weapon was appalled and horrified at what he'd done. But he saw something different in Riggs' eyes. Martin had seen it before in others, but never from a man like Riggs. Generals, and others like them, didn't look at someone like Martin that way. It was a look of respect. Not the kind of respect Martin gave to Riggs; the respect of a soldier to his commanding officer was required. This was earned respect. Respect because he'd done something Riggs could never do. He'd killed more men in one morning than Riggs had in his entire military life. Respect. Respect and fear are what Martin saw in Riggs' eyes, but he knew that would happen.

Riggs, the tall general, always the one imposing his will on those in the room with him, took a step back. He looked Martin up and down.

"They're all gone. We don't have to worry about an attack from them." Martin couldn't help but throw his head back and let out a laugh. "There's more armies coming. Three or four just to the north. They're not all here, but they're on the way. Word of what happened to Montgomery's army is moving up to the others. They assume it's a plague of some sort."

Martin concealed his joy as he recounted some of the details about the deaths of the rebel soldiers.

"Are you certain? About the armies I mean," Riggs' face changed and he became the confident General again after hearing information he didn't know about the enemy.

Martin nodded. "The only one that didn't die was sent to alert the other General of the situation. The others I spoke to said they were sure an attack wouldn't happen and that retreat was possible while they deal with and hopefully contain the plague." He smiled again but kept the laugher to himself this time.

Riggs turned and looked at the map of the ground they were on. Martin knew what the man was thinking, but Riggs confirmed it by asking the question.

"Armies to the north?" Riggs said.

"Yes, three or four I believe. But smaller than Montgomery's—much smaller than ours."

Riggs studied the map, Martin studied Riggs. He'd never been trained on such things but his time in service to his country taught him quite a bit. Riggs shook his head and looked back at Martin.

"They won't attack from anywhere north of where Montgomery's army is—was. This creek is too wide," he traced a finger over a part of the map. "They have to move in where Montgomery was and they won't because they know how big we are. Montgomery probably didn't stand a chance either. Smaller demoralized groups won't stand a chance either. It might not be what I had in mind, but it achieved the goal. Good work, Mr. Quigley."

Riggs lifted his arm as if he was going to pat Martin on the back, but stopped himself and turned away. Martin smiled. He still held power over him. He was afraid to touch him.

"General Riggs," Martin said, his words cold, "I think, given my value to the Union Army, I deserve a promotion."

"A promotion," Riggs laughed. "Why on earth would you get a promotion?"

"Anyone else who killed an entire army singlehandedly would be given medals. Awards. Meet the president and be sent home. I realize I'm still valuable and I understand that. But I want a promotion to fit with my importance to the army. That is, if you want me to stay. With no engagements in sight and my time with the army coming to a close, I could be on my way home soon. Or to Washington to see Lincoln. "

"So a promotion will keep you here. You won't leave when your time is up?"

Riggs pulled out a cigar, spun it.

"For the right job, yes."

"And what job is that, Mr. Quigley?"

"General."

"Mr. Quigley," Riggs smiled, close to a laugh but not quite. "There is training that is involved. You need to go to school and earn the title that way."

"There are field promotions. And I want to be General. I don't want your job, don't worry. I just want a title equal to my value. You're a General because you're more valuable than those men out there." Martin pointed a thumb behind him. "If one of them dies, the army goes on to fight another day. If you die there are all those years of training you just mentioned that go into filling your shoes. More training, more value. I don't have the training but my skills, like yours, are somewhat unique. We would be fighting and—again as you said—people would be dying today if it wasn't for me. All those men, and you, would be putting your lives at risk today or tomorrow if it wasn't for the work I did. The risk I took. I'm valuable the way you're valuable. Not the way *they* are valuable."

Silence stretched between them, lasting longer than what Martin thought was comfortable, but he'd said his peace and wasn't going to be the one to break it. Unlike the night with Mary-Louise, he wasn't going to make his move too soon.

More silence. Martin stood there. He had no idea what Riggs was thinking. Obviously, there was more to it than just making him a General. Yes, he could promote him. But there were ramifications outside of this tent that Riggs had to worry about. Martin didn't care about those. He was more powerful than Riggs or those who would judge him and therefore cared little about them. The silence persisted and then, finally, was broken.

"Here is my dilemma," Riggs said. "And it's obvious the relationship has changed between us. I'm fine with that. But here is the problem I'm running into in my head. I can make you a General, like you said through a field promotion. But if I don't have a good reason then they're going to toss me out and then you. That will be the end of it. I like you Martin, but we need to be smart about this. Others, the men above me, they know about you too. I want to be able give this to you. And I understand your point, and your value. But I can't do it without risking my post and my livelihood in the army." Riggs looked at Martin and Martin stared right back at him. He tried to get a read on his former superior officer. Then a flash in his eye, something there told Martin that Riggs was telling the truth.

"You have a family?" Martin asked.

Riggs looked confused and nodded.

"You need to take care of them. I get it." Martin frowned and nodded. "I'll go back to my tent and wait for orders in the morning with everyone else. I— I'll put my gloves back on too. If word gets out about the Rebs, no one will hear what happened from me."

Riggs nodded again. "I'm sorry I couldn't be more helpful, Martin."

Martin nodded again and pushed through the flap and out into the afternoon sun. He looked out at the men he'd once thought of as on his side in this war. The fact was, no one was on his side. There were a few men, Marshall, General Riggs, George Anderson and a few others who would survive the next twenty-four hours. But most of them wouldn't. They would all be asleep soon, then Decay's work would begin.

THE END

ABOUT THE EDITOR / PUBLISHER

Dawn Shea is an author and half of the publishing team over at D&T Publishing. She lives with her family in Mississippi. Always an avid horror lover, she has moved forward with her dreams of writing and publishing those things she loves so much.

D&T Previously published material:
    ABC's of Terror
    After the Kool-Aid is Gone

Follow her author page on Amazon for all publications she is featured in.
    Follow D&T Publishing at the following locations:
    Website
    Facebook: Page / Group
    Or email us here: dandtpublishing20@gmail.com

JOE SCIPIONE

Joe Scipione is the author of *Zoo: Eight Tale of Animal Horror, Mr. Nightmare* and *Perhaps She Will Die*. He lives in the suburbs of Chicago with his wife and two kids. He is a member of the Horror Writer's Association and a Senior Contributor and horror book reviewer at Horrorbound.net. When he's not reading or writing you can usually find him cheering on one of the Boston sports teams or walking around the lakes near his home. Find him on twitter: @joescipione0 or at www.joescipione.com

-- 1st ed.

DECAY by Joe Scipione

Book One in the Contact series

Edited by Patrick C. Harrison III

Cover by Don Noble

Formatting by J.Z. Foster

Decay

www.ingramcontent.com/pod-product-compliance
Lightning Source LLC
Chambersburg PA
CBHW030239180626
46810CB00008B/3200